50 STATES TO CELEBRATE

Celebrating
VIRGINIA
and WASHINGTON, D.C.

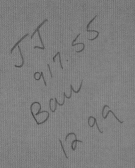

www.hmhbooks.com

The text of this book is set in Weidemann.
The display type is set in Bernard Gothic.
The illustrations are drawn with pencil and colored digitally.
The maps are pen, ink, and watercolor.

Photograph of American foxhound on page 32 © 2013 by Rob Evans as *Maggie* under
    Creative Commons license 2.0
Photograph of northern cardinal on page 32 © 2013 by Gregg Williams/Fotolia
Photograph of dogwood tree on page 32 © 2013 by April Robinson/Cutcaster

Library of Congress Cataloging-in-Publication Data
Bauer, Marion Dane.
Celebrating Virginia / by Marion Dane Bauer ; [illustrator, C. B. Canga].
p. cm. — (Green light readers. Level 3)
ISBN 978-0-544-04407-4 paper over board
ISBN 978-0-544-04417-3 trade paper
1. Virginia—Juvenile literature. I. Canga, C. B., ill. II. Title.
F226.3.B38 2013
975.5—dc23
2012039388

Manufactured in China
SCP 10 9 8 7 6 5 4 3 2 1
4500420701

50 STATES TO CELEBRATE

Celebrating
VIRGINIA
and WASHINGTON, D.C.

Written by **Marion Dane Bauer**
Illustrated by **C. B. Canga**

Houghton Mifflin Harcourt
Boston   New York

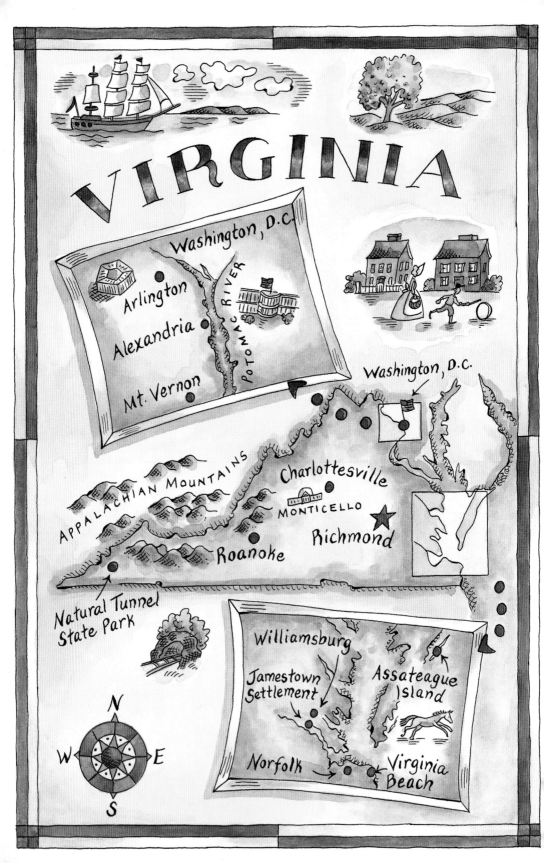

Hi! I'm Mr. Geo.

Did you know that the United States

began as 13 colonies?

Well, I'm in the state that was the first **colony.**

That's right! Virginia!

Let's find Virginia on the map.
It's right here on the Atlantic coast.

2

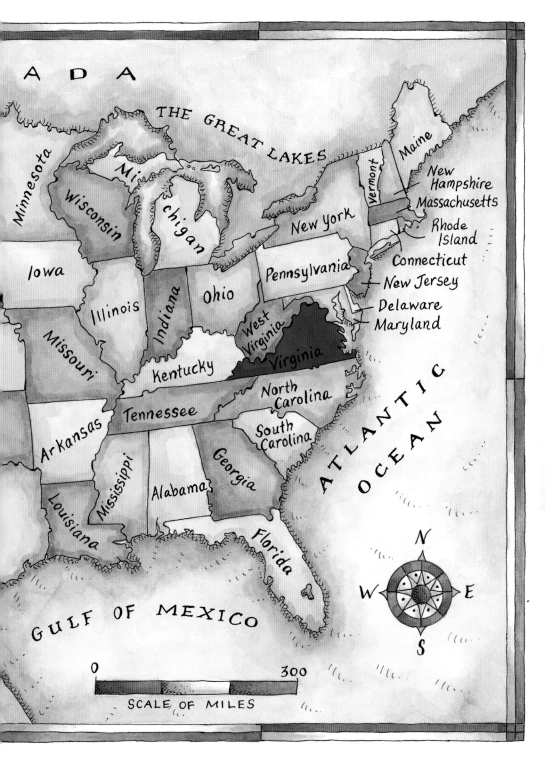

Look north of North Carolina.
Then look south of West Virginia and Maryland.
Great! You found it!

Have you ever seen a Tall Ship?
Here I am in a parade of
Tall Ships at the Norfolk
Harborfest.

These boats depend on wind to power their grand sails.

Modern navy **vessels** are part of the parade too.

I have the best view!

Virginia Beach is one of Virginia's biggest cities.

Many people come to visit its long, sparkling beach.

I like watching dolphins play in the waves.

I like to splash in the waves too!

Come on in!

I love ponies—don't you?

A herd of wild ponies live in Chinconteague

National Wildlife Refuge on nearby

Assateague Island.

When I bike there, I see them.

I really enjoy visiting the island during **Waterfowl** Week.

Look up! **Migrating** birds dot the sky.

The snow geese are my favorite.

Look below! Ducks and swans fill the marsh.

People have lived in Virginia for thousands of years.
The first people were Native Americans.
The English arrived about 400 years ago in 1607.
They built a settlement called Jamestown.
They were not prepared for the hard life in their new home.

Jamestown's first colonists arrived on three sailing ships—the *Susan Constant,* the *Godspeed,* and the *Discovery.*

Many settlers died of disease or starvation.
Probably all would have died without help.
Native Americans showed them new ways to
farm, fish, and hunt.
New settlers came with more food and supplies.
Jamestown grew stronger.

Pocahontas, daughter of the Native
American leader Powhatan, is still
remembered for helping the settlers.

We can experience what life was like in the
1770s at Colonial Williamsburg.
We can play the games colonial children played,
and taste the foods they ate.
Mmmm! Pretzel rolls and ginger cakes!

I like talking to the guides in costumes.
They dress and act like Virginians who
helped build our country.
I shook hands with Thomas Jefferson!
He wrote the **Declaration of Independence.**
And there's George Washington!
He led the army that won the **American Revolution.**
He was our first president, too.

At the Yorktown Victory Center, I can learn more about the American Revolution.
I see how the colonial army lived.
I even see cannons fire.
I love watching, but I don't like listening!

Did you know?

The **surrender** of British troops in Yorktown in 1781 led to the end of the American Revolution.

In Virginia, we can visit the homes of
past presidents.
There's Mount Vernon on the Potomac River.
That's where George Washington lived.
We can go to Monticello in Charlottesville too.
Thomas Jefferson lived there.

During the settlers' early years, most people lived by farming.
A Dutch ship brought the first enslaved Africans to Virginia.
Most were forced to work on big tobacco farms called **plantations**.
Many more ships followed.

Today, soybeans, corn, and cotton are important Virginia crops. Farmers here raise turkey and hogs, too.

The **Civil War** helped end slavery in our country in 1865.
The Northern states and the Southern states
fought against each other.
Many battles took place in Virginia.
There was much hardship on both sides.

Did you know?

The Southern general Robert E. Lee **surrendered** to the Northern general Ulysses S. Grant in the village of Appomattox Court House.

More than half of Virginia is covered with forests.
And visitors come from many places to hike in
the mountains.
The trails along Skyline Drive are beautiful.
They overlook the **fertile** Shenandoah Valley.

Fiddle music is a big tradition in the
Blue Ridge Mountains of Virginia.

I met a bear on the trail once, but we decided to go our separate ways!

Water has carved a tunnel in the Appalachian Mountains at Natural Tunnel State Park. It's so big that trains run through it!

Dinosaurs lived in Virginia long before people did.
The proof is in this rock **quarry.**
Look at all these dinosaur tracks!
They go in so many different directions.

More than 2,000 dinosaur tracks have
been found in Culpeper County, Virginia.

Dinosaurs no longer roam the earth.

But we can see life-size models of them at the

Kings Dominion theme park.

Yikes! That pack looks ready to attack!

Ancient forests lived and died in Virginia.
They were buried in the mountains and
turned into coal after many years.
Today, coal is a valuable source of energy.

NO SMOKING,
CARRYING MATCHES,
OR OPEN LIGHTS

SAFETY
FIRST

Miners work in deep, dark tunnels
to bring the coal to the surface.
It is a difficult job.
They work in tight spaces.
Elevators take them underground.
I wonder how far down this one goes!

Coal is fuel that can be used to
power a factory or cook food on a grill.

The city of Arlington is near our nation's capital.
It is full of important and historic places.
Many people visit Arlington National Cemetery
every year to honor those who died in our wars.

One grave at Arlington National Cemetery is
called the Tomb of the Unknown Soldier.

This five-sided building is called the Pentagon.
It is where the United States Department of Defense
does its job.
The people here work to protect our country.

Washington, D.C., is just across the Potomac River from Virginia.

It is the capital of the United States.

The headquarters of the **U.S. federal government** is located here.

Our president lives and works in the White House.

The White House has a rose garden and a vegetable garden.

The men and women in **Congress** make laws at the **U.S. Capitol.**

Judges make decisions about our laws in the **Supreme Court.**

EQUAL JUSTICE UNDER LAW

The Smithsonian in Washington, D.C., is the world's largest museum and research complex. It includes 19 museums and galleries.

Washington, D.C., is a great place for sightseeing.
The Lincoln Memorial and the Washington
Monument make me proud.
The Memorial to Martin Luther King Jr. does too.

And there are enough museums to keep me busy
for a long time!
I like the National Air and Space Museum best.

The history of our country began with Virginia.
Today, we can experience much of that history.
But Virginia is a modern place too.
It has big cities, busy ports, and
high-tech industries.

Virginia's natural beauty amazes me most, though.

Miles of coastline.

Miles of trout streams.

Miles of mountain trails.

Miles of country roads.

Virginia . . .

A great place to see, a great place to be!

Fast Facts
About Virginia

Nickname: Old Dominion

State motto: "Sic Semper Tyrannis" (Thus Always to Tyrants)

State capital: Richmond

Year of statehood: 1788

Other major cities: Alexandria, Charlottesville, Norfolk, Newport News, Roanoke, Virginia Beach

State dog: American foxhound

State bird: Northern cardinal

State flower: American dogwood

State flag:

Population: Approximately 8 million people, according to the 2010 census

Fun fact: Eight presidents were born in Virginia. They are George Washington (1st), Thomas Jefferson (3rd), James Madison (4th), James Monroe (5th), William Henry Harrison (9th), John Tyler (10th), Zachary Taylor (12th), and Woodrow Wilson (28th).

Dates in Virginia History

1600: Powhatan, a Native American leader, is the head of the Powhatan Confederacy, which includes about 30 Algonquian tribes.

1607: Jamestown founded by the Virginia Company of London.

1619: The first enslaved Africans are brought to Virginia.

1730: Settlers from **Europe** begin moving to western Virginia.

1775: The American Revolution begins.

1776: Thomas Jefferson writes the Declaration of Independence.

1781: British troops surrender at Yorktown.

1789: George Washington becomes the first president of the United States.

1861: Virginia **secedes** from the Union. The Civil War begins.

1863: Virginia's African American community gathers for the first Southern reading of Abraham Lincoln's **Emancipation Proclamation**.

1865: The Civil War ends.

1876: Coal is discovered in southwestern Virginia; the coal industry begins to grow.

1943: The Pentagon opens in Arlington, Virginia.

1990: Virginia elects the country's first African American governor—L. Douglas Wilder.

2001: A hijacked plane crashes into the Pentagon.

2007: The 400th anniversary of the founding of the Jamestown colony.

Activities

1. **LOCATE** the two states on Virginia's western border on the map on pages 2 and 3. Then, SAY each state's name out loud.

2. **DESIGN** a new license plate for Virginia. The license plate should have a picture and a short saying or phrase that tells something interesting about the state. Be creative and original, but leave room for the state name and the license plate numbers. On the back, write a sentence that explains why you created the design.

3. **SHARE** two facts you learned about Virginia with a family member or friend.

4. **PRETEND** you are at a Fourth of July party. The hosts are holding a trivia contest about Virginia because it was the very first colony. They plan to ask you and your team five questions. If you know the answers, your team wins.

   a. **WHEN** did the English first settle in Jamestown?

   b. **WHO** is the president who was born in Virginia and also wrote the Declaration of Independence?

   c. **WHAT** war helped end slavery in the United States?

   d. **WHAT** valuable source of energy comes from mines in Virginia?

5. **UNJUMBLE** these words that have something to do with Virginia. Write your answers on a separate sheet of paper.

   a. **LNOCYO** (HINT: Virginia was the first one)

   b. **LATL HPISS** (HINT: You can see some of these at Harborfest)

   c. **NHAWIGSTNO** (HINT: a president)

d. **COPANOHSAT** (HINT: a Native American who helped the colonists)

e. **TNYWOOKR** (HINT: Where the British surrendered during the American Revolution)

FOR ANSWERS, SEE PAGE 36.

Glossary

American Revolution: the war that won the 13 American colonies freedom from British rule; it took place from 1775–83. (p. 13)

ancient: old. (p. 22)

Civil War: the war between the Northern states and the Southern states that helped end slavery in the United States. (p. 17)

colony: a settlement ruled by another country. (p. 1)

Congress: the group of United States senators and representatives who are elected by people in their states to make national laws. There are two senators from each state. The number of representatives from each state varies because it is based on the number of people who live in the state. (p. 27)

Declaration of Independence: the formal document that stated the 13 colonies were free from British rule. (p. 13)

Emancipation Proclamation: a formal document issued by President Abraham Lincoln that freed slaves in the Southern states during the Civil War. (p. 33)

Europe: one of the seven continents in the world. Europe lies on the other side of the Atlantic from the East Coast of the United States. (p. 33)

fertile: good for plants to grow in. (p. 18)

migrating: moving from one place to another. (p. 9)

plantation: a large farm where crops are grown. (p. 16)

quarry: an open pit where stones and rocks are obtained by digging, cutting, or blasting. (p. 20)

secede: to withdraw membership. (p. 33)

Supreme Court: the highest court in the United States. There are nine judges on the Supreme Court. The Supreme Court also refers to the building where the judges work. (p. 27)

surrender: give up, also the act of giving up. (p. 14 & 17)

U.S. Capitol: the domed building in Washington, D.C., where Congress meets. (p. 27)

U.S. federal government: the government of the United States of America. The federal government includes three branches—the executive branch (the presidency); the legislative or lawmaking branch (Congress); and the judicial branch (the Supreme Court). (p. 26)

vessels: ships. (p. 5)

waterfowl: birds that live near the water, especially geese and ducks. (p. 9)

Answers to activities on page 34:

1) West Virginia and Kentucky; 2) drawings will vary; 3) answers will vary; 4a) 1607, 4b) Thomas Jefferson, 4c) the Civil War, 4d) coal; 5a) COLONY, 5b) TALL SHIPS, 5c) WASHINGTON, 5d) POCAHONTAS, 5e) YORKTOWN.